A New House for Little Mouse

By Cindy Wheeler
Illustrated by Stella Ormai

HAPPY HOUSE BOOKS
Random House, Inc.

Drip…drip…drip…

"I've had it!" Little Mouse cried as a large drop of water landed on his head. "This old house is leaky and full of holes. I need to move."

Little Mouse decided to talk to his friends Little Bird, Baby Bunny, and Big Bear. "They have nice houses," he thought. "They'll know how to help me find one too."

Everyone was gathered at the old oak tree, discussing the latest forest gossip.

"Hi, Little Mouse!" Big Bear called. "What's the news from your neck of the woods?"

"I'm house hunting, that's what," said Little Mouse.

"What happened to your house?" asked Little Bird.

"It's leaky and full of holes," Little Mouse explained.

"What Little Mouse means is that he's too lazy to fix up his *old* house," remarked Cranky Skunk.

"I'm not lazy!" snapped Little Mouse. "I just need a new house!"

"Why don't you stay with me?" said Big Bear.

"Or me!" chirped Little Bird.

"Or me!" begged Baby Bunny.

"I have an idea!" cried Little Mouse. "I will stay with *all* of you. I can see what your houses are like. Then I will know what kind of a house is right for me."

As soon as Little Mouse arrived at Big Bear's cave that night, he looked for a cozy place to sleep.

"I usually sleep over there," said Big Bear, pointing to the back of the cave. "Would you like this spot?" Big Bear pointed to a large empty place nearby.

Little Mouse took his pillow and blanket out of his suitcase and tried to make himself comfortable on the hard ground. Suddenly a loud rumble echoed through the cave. *R-o-a-rummmmmm!* Big Bear was snoring!

Little Mouse pulled his blanket over his ears, tucked his head under his pillow, and set his suitcase on top. But he could still hear it. *R-o-a-rummmmmm!*

In the morning Big Bear asked Little Mouse how he liked sleeping in a cave.

"You do have lots of room," said Little Mouse. "But I think I need a smaller house—with less echo!"

"Little Bird's nest is smaller," said Big Bear. "Maybe a nest is the right house for you."

When Little Mouse arrived at Little Bird's tree, Little Bird was searching for breakfast in the grass.

"Hi, Little Mouse! How was your night in Big Bear's cave?" he asked.

"To tell you the truth," said Little Mouse, "I didn't sleep a wink."

"You do look tired," said Little Bird. "Why don't you come home with me and take a nap?"

"What a wonderful idea!" Little Mouse sighed.

Then he
looked up.
There, on
the highest
limb of the
tallest tree
in the woods,
was Little
Bird's nest.
Little Mouse
had never
realized how
high up
it was.
    He tucked
his suitcase
under his
arm and
started
climbing.
    He
climbed
and he
climbed
and he
climbed.

Just as the sun was starting to set, Little Mouse
reached the nest. "There you are!" cried Little Bird.
"You're in time for dinner. I brought home *two* worms
today—one for you and one for me!"

"Oh, thank you, Little Bird," Little Mouse said,
eyeing the fat worms. "But if you don't mind, I might
just go to...to...to..."

Little Bird watched as Little Mouse dozed off.

In the morning Little Bird asked Little Mouse how he liked sleeping in a nest.

Little Mouse peered over the edge of the nest and blinked. It certainly was a long way down!

"You do have a beautiful view," said Little Mouse. "But I think I prefer a house that's closer to the ground."

"Baby Bunny's rabbit hole is *in* the ground," said Little Bird. "It might be just the thing."

Little Mouse spent the day climbing down the tree. That evening Baby Bunny found him resting on his suitcase outside the door of the rabbit hole.

"Hi, Little Mouse! How was your night in Little Bird's nest?" he asked.

"It was fine *in* the nest," answered Little Mouse. "But going up and coming down is for the birds!"

Baby Bunny took him inside the rabbit hole and introduced his fourteen brothers and sisters.

"I didn't know you had such a large family," said Little Mouse, politely shaking each bunny's paw and trying to remember all their names.

"I know you must be tired, Little Mouse," said Baby Bunny. "Here is a place to sleep." He pointed to a bed.

"What a nice big *guest* bed!" Little Mouse thought as he crawled into it. He was soon sound asleep. Suddenly he woke up with a *thump*! He opened his eyes. He was on the floor. His bed was full of bunnies!

He crawled back in. *Thump!* A big furry foot pushed him back out. He crawled back in. *Thump!* Another foot pushed him out again.

There were so many bunnies sleeping in the bed that every time one rolled over, Little Mouse rolled out.

In the morning Baby Bunny asked him how he liked sleeping in a rabbit hole.

"You do have a cozy house," said Little Mouse. "But I'm not used to so much company."

Little Mouse packed his suitcase and set off. He knew just where he wanted to go. He walked through the forest, past the old oak tree, right up to his own little house. He did not even stop to take off his jacket and scarf as he climbed into bed. He went right to sleep.

When he woke up, he
looked around. There were
no bunnies in his bed. He
was not up in a tree. There
were no snoring bears to
disturb the quiet.

"This is the right house
for me!" Little Mouse said.
"All it needs is some work."

Little Mouse spent the next week working
on his house.

He patched the holes
in the ceiling.

He cleaned the shelves.

He painted the walls.

When he was finished, he decided to have a party. He sent invitations to all his friends.

I'M HAVING A PARTY

and want you to see

THE PERFECT HOUSE

FOR A MOUSE LIKE ME

♡ L.M. ♡

That night everyone came to celebrate Little Mouse's new house.

"Why, this is your *old* house, Little Mouse," Baby Bunny said.

"It's my old house with no leaks and no holes, newly painted and cleaned," said Little Mouse. "It just needed fixing up."

"I've heard *that* before," said Cranky Skunk.

"Three cheers for Little Mouse and his *new* house!" said Big Bear.

After everyone went home, Little Mouse sank down in his chair by the fire. He was tired but happy.

"My friends do have wonderful houses," he thought. "A cave is a nice house for a bear, and a nest is a nice house for a bird, and a rabbit hole is a nice house for a bunny. But the nicest kind of house for me is...*my own*!"